W9-BYL-496

TIME HOP SWEETS SHOP

Brownies with
Benjamin Franklin

By J.L. Anderson
Illustrated by Sally Garland

Rourke
Educational Media
rourkeeducationalmedia.com

www.rourkeeducationalmedia.com

Edited by: Keli Sipperley
Cover and Interior layout by: Tara Raymo
Cover and Interior Illustrations by: Sally Garland

Library of Congress PCN Data

Brownies with Benjamin Franklin / J.L. Anderson
(Time Hop Sweets Shop)
ISBN (hard cover)(alk. paper) 978-1-68191-375-9
ISBN (soft cover) 978-1-68191-417-6
ISBN (e-Book) 978-1-68191-458-9
Library of Congress Control Number: 2015951488

Printed in the United States of America,
North Mankato, Minnesota

Dear Parents and Teachers,

Fiona and Finley are just like any modern-day kids. They help out with the family business, face struggles and triumphs at school, travel through time with important historical figures ...

Well, maybe that part's not so ordinary. At the Time Hop Sweets Shop, anything can happen, at any point in time. The family bakery draws customers from all over the map–and all over the history books. And when Tick Tock the parrot squawks, Fiona and Finley know an adventure is about to begin!

These beginner chapter books are designed to introduce students to important people in U.S. history, turning their accomplishments into adventures that Fiona, Finley, and young readers get to experience right along with them.

Perfect as read-alouds, read-alongs, or independent readers, books in the Time Hop Sweets Shop series were written to delight, inform, and engage your child or students by making each historical figure memorable and relatable. Each book includes a biography, comprehension questions, websites for further reading, and more.

We look forward to our time travels together!

Happy Reading,
Rourke Educational Media

Table of Contents

Fire Fighting

Finley came up with a new idea—a brownie cupcake with chocolate cookie dough icing!

If he could pull it off, he might win a blue ribbon at the Old Town fair tomorrow.

"You'll be Cupcake King of the World," Fiona said.

This sounded super sweet!

Fiona and Finley mixed the brownies. The smell of chocolate tickled their noses.

Finley filled the baking pan extra full. He wanted the brownies to be big.

"Oops," Fiona said. She spilled some batter on the pan.

Mom was helping someone in the family's Sweets Shop. Their parrot, Tick Tock, chirped.

The customer handed Mom a hundred dollar bill for two dessert trays.

"Pay day! Pay day!" Tick Tock squawked.

Finley saw the picture of Benjamin Franklin on the big bill.

Mom gave the customer some change. Then she rushed to set the pan in the oven for the kids.

Fiona set the timer. At least she thought she did.

Soon, the sweet smell in the shop left. The place began to stink.

"Smoke!" Finley yelled.

The fire alarms went off. Tick Tock screeched.

Fiona could hardly think. She grabbed a fire extinguisher and handed it to Mom.

Mom opened the oven. The brownies were on fire!

Mom sprayed everywhere. Smoke filled the air.

Finley thought he heard sirens. He saw the blue and red fire truck lights a moment later.

"You did the right thing," a firefighter told Mom. Then the firefighter team left.

Thank goodness everything was okay! The brownies were ruined, though.

"I should've paid more attention," Mom said.

Fiona looked at the timer she forgot to set. "Me too."

Finley had to start all over again.

"Don't feel bad," Fiona said. "At least we got to meet the fire department."

Well, that part was neat.

Finley thought of the one-hundred dollar bill again.

"Do you remember reading about how Benjamin Franklin started the first fire department?" Finley asked.

"And he started a library so people could borrow books," Fiona said.

"Good thing the idea caught on for fire departments and libraries," Dad said. He set his glasses down on the table.

Fiona and Finley helped Mom and Dad clean up.

"Big mess! Big mess!" Tick Tock said.

Fiona wished the bird knew how to scrub the oven.

Finley made a new batch of brownie cupcakes. This time, he made them smaller.

Mom checked things over before she set the new batch in the oven.

There wasn't much time left before bedtime and the fair was the next morning!

Fiona set the timer. She double checked it to be sure.

The Sweets Shop began to smell like yummy chocolate again.

Finley thought of winning the blue ribbon.

Then there was a loud POP!

The lights in the shop flickered. And then the power went out.

The brownie cupcakes only had a few more minutes to bake.

Fiona clapped her hands like it might turn the power back on. Nothing happened.

"I think the oven shorted the power," Dad said.

Mom might've nodded. There was no way to tell because it was dark in the Sweets Shop.

"The power should come back on in a minute," Mom said.

A minute went by. Fiona clapped again. The power was still gone.

So was Finley's blue ribbon dream.

"Your dad and I will figure this out," Mom said. "Hang tight with Tick Tock."

"We could use Benjamin Franklin's help," Fiona said. "He knew a lot about electricity."

Finley heard the siren again, only it was the bell above the side door jingling.

"Look at the time! Look at the time!" Tick Tock squawked.

This meant someone special was about to visit.

A man with long hair and a funny old-fashioned suit walked into the dark shop. He carried a small lamp. "Good evening," he said.

Fiona liked his accent.

All Finley could do was stare! "You're Benjamin Franklin," he stammered.

"Please call me Ben," the man said.

"You look younger and less plump in person," Fiona said.

Benjamin Franklin laughed. "Honesty is the best policy, I suppose."

He sniffed the air. "Something smells delicious!"

Finley told him about the brownie cupcakes ... and the fire.

"I've made some mistakes, too," Ben said. "I tried to cook a turkey but ended up zapping myself instead."

Finley was starting to feel much better.

Electrified!

Ben checked out the oven using his lamp. "I made a stove in my day, but it was like a fireplace," he said.

"The Franklin Stove," Fiona said. She was proud she remembered.

Ben clapped he was so pleased. The power went on and off for him.

The oven was still warm when Ben opened it. "May I try one of these?" he asked.

Where were Finley's manners? With Ben's help, he served them all a treat.

The brownie cupcakes were extra gooey because of the power outage.

Ben licked his fingers clean. "These are fit for a king! When I was young, I only ate bread and drank water for some meals."

After they ate, Ben explored the kitchen.
Fiona tried to turn on the light for him
even though the power was still out. "Sorry
it is so dark," she said.

"I like the dark," said Ben. "Such a good
time to read and think."

Ben found Dad's glasses. The top half helped him see far away. The bottom half helped him see up close.

"Bifocals look a bit different now from when I invented them," Ben said.

"You've done so many things," Finley said. He could hardly believe he was in the presence of such a great inventor.

Plus, Ben was one of the Founding Fathers of the United States!

"I've learned a few things that would be fun to show you," Ben said.

"We'd love that!" Fiona said.

"Time is too precious to waste," Ben said. "Let's visit Philadelphia in the mid-1700s."

The hands on the clock turned around.

The room began to spin.

Fiona cheered. She loved time travel!

Finley liked the adventures, just not getting dizzy.

Splash! They landed in a pond wearing old-fashioned swimsuits. The sun was bright, but the water in Philadelphia was cold.

Finley was happy he'd taken swim lessons. Fiona splashed around.

"Here," Ben said. "Hang on to these."

Fiona and Finley grabbed two kites from Ben. A gust of wind picked up.

"Now swim!" Ben said with a laugh.

They sailed across the pond.

"Whee!" Fiona squealed.

Finley laughed, too. What fun!

When they took a break, Ben showed them hand fins. He designed them when he was just a boy.

"I almost opened a swimming school in London," Ben said. "Many people wanted me to teach them to swim when I lived there."

"I'm glad you didn't or our lives might be much different," Finley said.

"Yeah," Fiona said. "You helped America become free."

"Things worked out for the best," Ben said.

The three of them dried off. Ben told them how he was the only Founding Father to sign all the papers to free the United States.

Fiona hoped to do half as many things as Ben when she grew up.

Next, Ben grabbed one of the kites.

"This helped me understand more about electricity," he said.

The day changed from sunny to stormy. They were suddenly in a field, wearing suits.

Rain started coming down.

"Ahh! I love a good storm," Ben said.

Ben tied a silk ribbon to an iron key. Then he tied the kite to the key. The string to the kite was wet.

"Here," Ben said to Fiona. "You can fly this."

"Fiona won't get hurt, will she?" Finley asked. He didn't want anything bad to happen to his sister.

"You're just jealous that I get to hold the kite," she said.

"Not true," Finley said. Maybe it was a little true. This was a legendary moment.

Lightning lit up the sky.

Fiona gasped. She didn't want to get struck.

She let go of the silk ribbon.

A gust of wind sailed the kite away.

How much would the future change if they couldn't get the kite back?

Even vocabulary about electricity might not be the same. The idea was so new at the time that Benjamin Franklin made his own words up.

Finley raced after the runaway kite.

Fiona bolted like the lightning in the sky.

Near-Fiasco at the Franklin House

Rain sprinkled.

Fiona and Finley kept running.

Fiona jumped and caught the tail of the silk ribbon.

The clouds created a charge down the wet string. The key nearly glowed when it sent a shock to Ben's hand.

Electricity!

The shock made Finley think of the time he slid around in socks and then touched a doorknob.

They hid in a small shed while it rained.

Ben told them more about electricity and things like charges and batteries.

The rain let up enough to walk to Ben's home. Thunder boomed.

It was a two-story house with red brick. The place looked like some of the buildings in Old Town.

Finley spotted a lightning rod on the chimney. It matched the one at the top of the Sweets Shop.

"I made the rod to test things and to keep the house safe from lightning," Ben said.

Fiona liked the idea of being safe after the kite mess. The storm was getting worse.

Ben's wife, Deborah, met them by the front door. Ben kissed her on the cheek. "Hello, dear. Meet Fiona and Finley."

"Hello!" She brought them towels to dry off.

Ben gave them each a tart. "This is one of my favorite things to eat. It is not as good as your brownies, though."

Fiona and Finley smiled.

Finley could've spent a week looking around the house. There were all sorts of newspapers.

"Those are from my days as a printer," Ben said. He showed them stacks of his writings.

"You must write all of the time," Fiona said.

Ben nodded. "I try to write things worth reading about."

Fiona was careful not to drop some of the printing stuff. She found a suit in the corner of the room.

"That's for my work with the postal system," Ben said.

"Is there anything you don't do?" Finley asked.

"Sleep in," Deborah said. She winked at Ben.

Fiona and Finley thought about getting up earlier when they got home.

Finley wasn't as careful as his sister. He pulled a book off of a crowded shelf.

Uh oh!

Ben covered his eyes.

The book fell down onto a wooden case with glass bowls.

CLANG!

Finley was happy the bowls didn't break. "Sorry," he said.

"Accidents happen from time to time," Ben said. "This is a musical instrument I made that I call the glass armonica."

Ben played music for them. The humming glass sounded pretty!

"I invented many things, but this is my favorite personally," Ben said. "You two must find something you love to do."

Just then, sparks lit up the house! The sound of thunder shook the walls.

"Oh no! Not more fire," Fiona said.

"Lightning struck the rod," Ben said. "We'll be fine."

He showed them his test. Electricity flowed through the lightning rod down to a glass tube before traveling outside.

Bells rang. Lights flashed.

Fiona and Finley didn't touch a thing.

"I get tired of these ringing bells and flashing lights when Ben travels," Deborah said.

Ben kissed her cheek again. "You've been such a huge help to me."

Then Ben turned to Fiona and Finley. "I'm so glad you could join me today."

"Thank YOU," they said together.

Before they left Philadelphia over two-hundred years ago, Ben said, "Do not fear mistakes. You will know failure. Continue to reach out."

Fiona and Finley took those words in.

"Welcome home!" Tick Tock said when they returned. The lights flashed back on.

Fiona and Finley would try to try the new brownie cupcake with cookie dough frosting recipe another day.

For now, the gooey brownies would do. To Benjamin Franklin, they were blue ribbon winning brownies. No reward could be any sweeter.

About Benjamin Franklin

Benjamin Franklin, one of the Founding Fathers of the United States, was born into a large family on January 17, 1706, in colonial Boston. He was one of seventeen children! When he was ten years old, Benjamin Franklin stopped going to school and he was supposed to learn to be a candle and soap  maker like his father. He grumbled about that, so instead Benjamin worked as an apprentice for his brother who owned a print shop. The two argued and Benjamin's brother was sometimes mean to him. Benjamin then went to Philadelphia, where he worked for a printer. After traveling to London, he later opened his own print business and wrote many things.

As his business boomed, Benjamin Franklin became more involved in his community. He organized the first volunteer fire-fighting club. He helped establish a hospital and a lending library. He also helped get roads paved and street lamps lit. These ideas spread to other cities. Benjamin

Franklin served as postmaster general to the colonies and improved the way mail was delivered.

Benjamin Franklin was fascinated with the world. As he told Fiona and Finley, he didn't like to waste time. He read lots of books to learn new ideas and languages. He invented many things, including bifocals, the first American musical instrument (the glass armonica), the Franklin Stove, and the lightning rod. His experiments in electricity were groundbreaking and made him famous. Instead of Fiona and Finley helping him in the famous kite experiment, his twenty-one year old son William was actually his assistant, who is often wrongly illustrated as a little boy in accounts about Benjamin's discoveries.

This gifted thinker traveled widely and spent almost a third of his life overseas. He used his diplomatic skills to sign treaties with other countries and help America win independence from Britain. He signed the Declaration of Independence, the Treaty of Paris, and the U.S. Constitution. Benjamin Franklin lived a full life until the time of his death in Philadelphia on April 17, 1790. His funeral was attended by 20,000 people and thousands of people a year still visit his grave, many tossing pennies for good luck.

Comprehension Questions

1. How did Fiona almost ruin the famous kite experiment?

2. What was Benjamin Franklin's personal favorite invention, and what did Finley do to almost ruin it?

3. List at least three of Benjamin Franklin's contributions or inventions.

Websites to Visit

www.libertyskids.com/
    arch_who_bfranklin.html

www.pbs.org/benfranklin/explore.html

www.sciencekids.co.nz/electricity.html

Q & A with J.L. Anderson

What did you find challenging while writing this story?
Benjamin Franklin was such an interesting man who did such interesting things that I wanted to keep researching his life, legacy, and his inventions. Research is a great thing, but at some point, a writer needs to trust that he or she has enough information and get the actual writing done!

Were there any surprises in your research?
I had no idea how much I would enjoy reading parts of Benjamin Franklin's autobiography. I thought Benjamin Franklin's childhood was particularly interesting, such as how he was an early reader but struggled in arithmetic. He seemed to have a good sense of humor and there were a few times I laughed aloud, like when he described his "awkward, ridiculous appearance" the day he met his future wife. He was a mess from traveling and was carrying two puffy rolls of bread under his arms and had his mouth full while he was eating the third roll.

What advice do you think Benjamin Franklin would give to young people today?
I think he would stress the importance of reading and writing. He was only in school two years, and he educated himself by reading books. His love of reading created friendships and shaped the future.
Benjamin Franklin took his father's writing advice and studied and copied some of the books he liked as a way to grow as a writer. He and a group of writers would gather and critique each other's work. Later, his writing helped him land jobs. He wrote that his ability to write gave him many advantages. His writing skills even influenced the United States when he helped write documents like the Declaration of Independence.

About the Author

J. L. Anderson enjoys writing, but if given the chance, she would love to own a Sweets Shop with the bonus of time travel! If she had to pick just one sweet treat, she might choose chocolate or ice cream though usually not chocolate ice cream (just plain vanilla or strawberry).You can learn more about J.L. Anderson at www.jessicaleeanderson.com.

About the Illustrator

Sally Anne Garland was born in Hereford England and moved to the Highlands of Scotland at the age of three. She studied Illustration at Edinburgh College of Art before moving to Glasgow where she now lives with her partner and young son.